Billy's Amazing Story

By Black Bart Jim

Proisle Publishing Service

1177 Avenue of the Americas, 5th Floor, New York, NY 10036, USA

info@proislepublishing.com

ISBN: 978-1-7370435-4-6 (sc)

Billy's Amazing Story

By Black Bart Jim

Billy's Journey Starts Here

It was just after the war in 1945, young Billy was playing on one of the many bombsites, like most of the kids did in those days. He was routing around in the rubble, when he saw a large blue stone, it was the size and shape of a rugby ball.

Now, who was Billy? He was a fourteen year old orphan of the war, living by his wits, he was very determined not to finish up in an orphanage. He would never settle in one place for too long. Like many others he was living on the edge of the law, just one jump ahead of the authorities. Not a criminal, just doing what had to be done to survive. Rescuing tasty little morsels and visiting the charitable food kitchens, for a hot meal. Not the best of things, but he was a free spirit, that's how he liked it. Well, that is until he found the stone.

Billy wasn't sure what he had found, but he knew someone who might, old Ted. the tramp. He used to be a professor before the war, but the blitz unhinged him, he was quite happy living the way he was. So, Billy wrapped the stone in an old bit of cloth he had found, and then made his way to where old Ted would be.

"Hello Billy" said old Ted, "what have you got there?". "Dun no", said Billy, "that's why I brought it for you to look at. It looks like some sort of very smooth stone". Old Ted unwrapped the stone, "Well. I don't think it's a stone Billy", he said. "It looks more like an egg, and quite an old one at that. Where did you find it?" Billy told him. Then old Ted scratched his head and said, "There used to be some rum old characters living up there before the war. Archaeologists, I think they were", he put the egg down, "Do you want a cup of tea Billy? I just put the kettle on". Billy nodded, "Yes please".

Billy said, "you sure it's an egg?". "Sure, as I can be", said old Ted, "tell you what, I'm still in touch with some of my old university friends. One of them taught archaeology, I'll take this along and show it to him, and see what he says". They sat drinking their tea and chatting about things in general. Then Billy said it was time for him to go. He asked old Ted to let him know, as soon as he had any information.

Billy was thinking it was about time he changed his abode. As this was the second time the local bobby had nearly caught him. Billy was just mooching around by Camden Town Tube Station. When little Jack came up to him and said, "Old Ted asked me to give you a message. He says he's got some answers for you, any time you're ready pop up and see him". "Thanks Jack," said Billy, "I'll make my way up to see him now". He made his way up to College Street, keeping an eye out for that crafty old copper, on the way.

When Billy reached old Ted's place, old Ted said, "Sit down I've got some exciting news to tell you". Billy sat down and said, "OK, tell us all about it". "Don't start laughing when I tell you what I've found out", said Ted. "My friend has been into archaeology for a long time, so he should know what he is talking about". "Alright Ted, I promise, don't keep me in suspense, tell me what you found out?". "Well, it appears that what you have found is an egg, not just any ordinary egg, but a very special one". "Come on", Billy says as he starts to giggle, but stops just in time, when he sees Ted's face very serious. Then says, "Ted don't keep me in the dark, what is it?"

"A dragon's egg, now don't laugh you promised". "I'm not laughing Ted, I think it's great. Come on he must have told you more, or you wouldn't be buzzing like a hive of bees". "Right young man, let me get my thoughts in order, then I'll tell you all about it", said old Ted. "My friend told me, years ago he came across these old tablets with strange writing on them. This turned out to be runes, an ancient language. He studied them for years, till he finally managed to decipher and translate them. The story they told was absolutely fantastic". "Come on Ted spit it out, I'm nearly wetting myself with anticipation", said Billy.

"Right", said Ted, "sit back and be prepared to be amazed". "Back in the days of the dinosaurs, dragons also lived. When the dinosaurs died out the dragons didn't. In fact, there were still records of them right up to the Middle Ages. In the early days of man, dragons and men lived side by side in peace. In fact, dragons were looked upon as 'luck bringers'. As man developed, dragons were looked upon as a nuisance, this was because they occupied some of the best land, and as usual man wanted it for their own. So, every time a house burnt down after being struck by lightning, or animals were found dead on the moors. They used these as excuses to blame the dragons, and started hunting them down to extinction or so they thought".

"Some managed to hide away from man up in the Fells in the Yorkshire Dales, that area between Lancashire and also spreads over a fare part of Yorkshire. It would appear that at the beginning of the war, the dragons took umbrage to Nazi Germany bombing our cities, and would come out and attack lone bombers, when they had the chance. These stories were told by German airmen, after they were captured and put into POW camps. Telling how they were knocked out of the sky, by flying monsters. Everyone put this down to these airmen, believing their own German propaganda, that they were unbeatable. They could not face the truth, that they were".

"At least, this is my friend's theory. There had been some reported sightings, of flying objects late at night, but these were put down to the amount of alcohol in the person reporting the sighting. He has a theory that somewhere up there some dragons still live. This egg may have been laid by an overzealous pregnant dragon chasing a German bomber. The eggs can lay dormant for years before hatching, or so the translation says. He suggests if it is possible, that the egg be returned to the Dales. There you are young man, what do you think of that?"

"I'm finding it a bit hard to take it all in, but I agree that the egg belongs back in the Dales. Being an orphan myself I know how it would feel to hatch out and find none of your own kind around. The question is how do we get it back to the Dales, where ever they may be. As I found it, I feel it is my duty to be the one to return it". "Don't you worry about that Billy, I have a friend with a narrowboat who works on the canals, taking goods north and bringing goods south. In fact, he's birthed at Regents Park canal at the moment, waiting for a shipment to go north. As it's only up the road, why don't we pop up and see him now?" "A good idea", said Billy. With that they both made their way up to the Regents Canal.

They walked along the towpath until old Ted stopped by one of the boats. There was a man who was busy washing down the deck with a mop. "Good Morning Sid", said old Ted. "Why if it isn't Ted, how are you me old mucca?" "Fine Sid, I have a little favour to ask", "Fire away Ted only too pleased to help", said Sid.

"This young lad, Billy, needs to go up to the Yorkshire Dales. So that he can return something; that has been missing from there for a while". "Sure, I'd be only too pleased to help. In fact, my last delivery is to the town of Skipton, which leads to the Dales".

"Come on board, I'll put kettle on". Ted and Billy followed Sid into his cabin. They sat down and made themselves comfortable, while Sid made some tea. Sid said he would be loading the boat tomorrow morning. If Billy could be there by twelve, they could make a start soon after. They stayed on the boat for a couple of hours. As they left, Billy said he'd be back at twelve sharp tomorrow. They made their way back to Ted's place, and Ted told Billy to go back to his place, and bring his things over to him, for safe keeping while he was away.

Billy was gone for about half an hour, he asked Ted if he could spend the night there. This was because that crafty copper almost caught him this time. Ted said it was alright, Billy stored his belongings at Ted's place. Then they both got comfortable and settled down for the rest of the evening.

The next day, Billy packed all that he was taking with him, he made sure that the egg was safe and secure. He said goodbye to Ted and thanked him for all his help, then made his way to the Regents Canal. By twelve o'clock everything was all stowed away and Billy was off, (though he didn't know it) to an adventure of his life.

Sid's boat had a diesel engine, so there wasn't the problem of hitching a horse. From the Regent canal they joined the Grand Union and made their way north, towards Birmingham, stopping just outside Rickmansworth for the night. Before settling down for the night, Billy made sure that the egg was safe, then he and Sid sat talking until it was time for bed.

The journey took just over eight days, traversing many canals. Birmingham & Fazeley, Trent & Mersey, Sheffield & South Yorkshire and Leeds & Liverpool, to name but a few. Stopping off at such places as, Braunston Junction, Oxford, Trent River Junction, Torksey Junction and Cross Keys, Yorkshire.

When they docked at Skipton, Sid saw to the unloading of his cargo. He found it would probably be another week, before there was any cargo for him to take down south. He told Billy he had a week to kill, and said, "How would it be if I hired a horse and cart, and took you up to the Dales?" "That'll be great", said Billy, "if it's not putting you out that is". "Nonsense I'd only be kicking my heals waiting for the cargo, besides I've never been there".

"Great", said Billy, "when can we get going?" "Steady on, we'll rest up for the night and be fresh to start tomorrow. I'll just go and see about the horse and cart, you just go and see if you can rustle up something to eat". When Sid got back, they tucked in to beans on toast and a pot of tea and some biscuits to dunk into the tea. Then they settled down for the night, ready for a fresh early start in the morning.

The next morning, they were off bright and early. Sid said "Well where are we heading for?" "I don't know", said Billy, "all I know is there will be, hills, valleys and caves". "That just about covers the whole of this area", said Sid, "any specific part you can think of?" "No, we just keep going, I think I'll know when we get there". said Billy. "Just remember, I've only got a week, so if we've found nothing in five days, I'll be heading back to the canal". "That's OK, you just drop me off if you've got to come back, and I'll just carry on looking", said Billy.

Sid looked at him and said, "Now, just hold it there, that's a big piece of country out there, it seems that what you've come up here to do, you're going to do it no matter what. So, I'll make a deal with you, we go back with the horse and cart, load you up with provisions, and give you some money. What do you say? any arguments and we get on the boat and head back south".

Billy looked him in the eye and said, "But how am I going to pay you back?" "We'll work that out when we come to it", said Sid "you could come and work on my boat to pay off the debt. What do you say?" "If it's the only way to finish what I started, it's a deal", Billy spat in the palm of his hand, and shook hands with Sid on the deal. "Right let's get started", said Sid.

They spent the first three days riding up hills, then down into valleys, and peering into every cave they came across, they must have travelled hundreds of miles. Billy said, "I think you're right Sid". "Ah, what about?" said Sid coming out of his daydreaming. "Me thinking, that I would come up here and know exactly where to go", Billy said, "It looks like I'm going to have to take you up on your offer". He reached into the cart to check if the egg was alright, it felt much warmer than usual.

Billy thought I wonder, then he said, "Sid can we try something?" "What?" said Sid. "The next turning, take it and stop after ten minutes". "Sure, why?" said Sid. "Call it a hunch", said Billy. When they reached the turning it was on the left, ten minutes later Sid stopped, when Billy checked the egg, it was warmer. Billy said, "Just keep going this way", they carried on till they came to a cross road, "Which way Billy?" "Straight ahead for ten minutes", said Billy, ten minutes later Billy checked the egg again, it was slightly cooler, "Back up and we'll take the right hand turning and stop after ten minutes". This they did and Billy checked the egg again, it was warmer. They carried on in this way, every time they came to a cross road or turning, by the time they stopped for the night, the egg was considerably warmer.

Billy knew he was on the right track, but he didn't build his hopes too high for he wasn't sure how much further they had to go. That night as he was dropping off to sleep, he could hear a voice in his head, calling his name,

'*Billy, Billy, Billy*' he tossed and turned trying to shut the voice up. '*Please don't ignore me Billy, I have to tell you something, please Billy*' "What do you want", '*Good you're listening*' "Get on with it". He looked over at Sid, who was fast asleep snoring, Billy was getting a little annoyed. '*Please Billy, have a little patience and all will be explained. If you carry on in the same direction you are travelling for approximately half a day tomorrow all will be revealed, until tomorrow then, good night Billy*'.

Billy lay thinking about what he had just heard as he gradually fell asleep again. In the morning, Billy told Sid all about the voice, and what it had told him. "Right the sooner we have breakfast the sooner we can be on our way", said Sid.

They had been travelling nearly five hours when Billy heard a voice. '*Billy you can tell your friend to stop now, and please neither of you be afraid at what you will see, we mean you no harm*'. Billy told Sid all that the voice had told him, he wasn't to worry, they would be perfectly safe, so they sat and waited, but not for long. All of a sudden there was a whoosh and it got darker over the wagon, then a large green dragon, appeared on the road in front of them.

Sid had the quick wit to jump down and calm the horse, before it had a chance to bolt, though it took a lot of doing. '*Sorry about that, tell your friend we are giving out calming vibrations to the horse, he should be OK to let go of now*', Billy passed the message onto Sid. Then Billy heard another voice, '*I believe you have brought something of mine back, which I was silly enough to lose some time ago. If you can place it on the rock over there, all will be revealed, as I said last night.*

Billy did as the dragon asked and was amazed at how much hotter the egg felt. Sid was staring at the dragon opened mouthed in astonishment, Billy nudged him and told him he was catching flies. Then his attention was drawn to a sound from where he had put the egg, the shell was in pieces and there sat a little red dragon. *'The spitting image of his farther',* said the green dragon, *'you do realise, that you and he are bonded for life, don't you Billy? That is the reason I can communicate with you, blood relatives and all that'.*

All the while Billy is telling this to Sid, to keep him in the picture. Sid and the green dragon, can see a big problem happening here and it needs to be sorted soon. It's alright while the red dragon is small and can't get around, but they didn't think London would appreciate a large red dragon flying around the town. They both thought it best, if Billy went back to London and hope that the bond weakens.

Billy said "Wait a minute, nobody asked what I want, I'm an orphan, I have no living relatives, Ruffus, that's what I've named him, is the nearest thing I have to a brother, I think I can get used to living up here". Sid said, "Look Billy you haven't thought this through, how are you going to support yourself, where and what are you going to live on.

This is not London where you can go to a charitable kitchen for a free meal, plus the fact that these dragons have managed to stay hidden from humans for thousands of years, you could spoil all this for them". *He's right, and you know it Billy, maybe when you are older and can fend for yourself better, but for the time being, going back home is best'.*

"Alright", said Billy, "you're both right, come on Sid let's get back to the canal, so we can make our way back home. I shall miss the little feller, but I suppose it's for the best". They said goodbye to the dragons and told them their secret was safe with them, and set off back to Skipton. Arriving at the same time as the cargo, so they quickly loaded the boat and set off back to London.

When they arrived back at the Regents Canal, over a week later, old Ted was waiting with an officious pompous looking gentleman, in a black overcoat and bowler hat. "Billy", said Ted, "some fantastic news, you're rich beyond compare, I'll let this gentleman fill you in. Sir, this is Billy or William as you prefer to call him. Billy this is a swank solicitor who represents your late Grandfather".

They shook hands and the swank solicitor introduced himself as, Allan Brodie Ewan McColl, acting for your late grandfather. "Master William Forte, the third, I have the pleasure in telling you, as the only living heir, to William Henry Havelock Forte, the first, and father of, William George James Forte, the second, and father of, William Forte the third, which is you. You inherit all your grandfathers' wealth". As Billy and the others pick themselves up off the floor, so to speak. Mr McColl carries on, "Now, who do you wish to be your guardians and trustees until you reach the age of twenty one?"

"Old Ted and Sid here, they may not look much but both have watched my back and looked out for me, saw to it that I stayed on the straight and narrow", said Billy. "Very well Master William, I will have the papers drawn up, if you would all care to pop along to my office tomorrow at ten o'clock at Lincolns Inn, to sign the papers. Good day to you gentlemen, I'll see you tomorrow at ten". He raised his bowler hat turned and left.

Old Ted said, "Great news, shall I call you William or what, and what's the first thing you plan to do?" "I think I can answer that" said Sid, "a small unobtrusive little place in the Yorkshire Dales, right Billy?" "Right Sid" said Billy, "and that will do nicely for me, and old Ted, Billy's still my name".

The next day the three chums, all cleaned and spruced up, presented themselves at the solicitors' office, at ten o'clock on the dot, they signed all the necessary papers. Then went to celebrate with a pie and mash dinner in Chapel Street Market. Sid told Ted all that went on up in the Dales. While Billy planned his intended future living with the dragons, which he couldn't wait to do.

Would you like to know something strange? In Skipton, yes, there is such a place, it's not just a building society, there is a brewery called 'The Copper Dragon Brewery', who's emblem or logo, call it what you may, just happens to be a green dragon (cross my heart and hope to die).

Billy and his Dragon

Now Billy was financially stable, he told his only two friends, he would like for them to join in a partnership, in a canal haulage company. Sid had the narrowboat, Ted had the brains and he had the money. He was not going to take no for an answer, they had been the only ones to show him kindness and compassion. Besides they were now his legal guardians, and Billy being shrewd, could see this as a way of keeping supplies being delivered to his new place in the Yorkshire Dales, without creating too much suspicion.

So, he took them both along to see the solicitor in Lincolns Inn, to make it all legal and above board.

"Well, what are you going to call yourselves?" the solicitor asked, "I hadn't given that a thought", said Billy. "How about, Bill, Sid & Ted? no! or maybe B.S.T.? no! I've got it, Sidney W. Edwards, yes that's it, what do you say?" Sid and Ted looked at one another, and said, "Where did that come from?" "I thought something posh would sound just right, Sidney for Sid, Edward for Ted, and W. for William", said Billy. "Sounds like a very good name to me", said Mr

McColl. "Just give me time to set the wheels in motion and set the paperwork up. When it's all ready, you can come in and sign the papers and you'll be up and running, so to speak".

"Yes, that sounds great", said Billy. "If you don't mind me butting in Billy", said Ted, "Sir would you care to act for the company as its legal representative if that's alright with you Billy". "Sure", said Billy, "you're the brains of the company, I'd never have thought of that. It would be a great idea".

"Thank you, very much young sir,", said the solicitor, "I will put it into action at the same time, as I am dealing with rest of your transactions. I think that concludes all the business, I'll bid you farewell and look forward to seeing you again, when everything is ready to be signed. Good day to you gentlemen". They bid him good day as each of them shook hands with him and left the office.

After everything had been signed and sealed, Billy rented a warehouse in Skipton and employed a couple of locals to run it for him. With his legitimate cargo, he would smuggle building material and store it in the warehouse. To be transported late at night when no one was around, up to the spot in the Dales where he intended to build his house, not so much a house, more a conversion of a cave into comfortable living space, for himself, and also, a large cavern for the Ruffus the dragon to live. This way, making it undetectable to nosey parkers.

The cave he had chosen was shielded from view by a clump of trees, with a fast flowing steam which flowed past the cave opening. His intention to build a waterwheel and attach it to two ex-army generators, which he had acquired with Sid's help. One to be held as a standby and to alternate there use every six months. This should provide enough electricity for, lighting, heating and any other power needed.

The work took some time as he could trust no one but Sid to help him and Sid could only offer him a week here and there, while he was waiting for cargo at Skipton. It also gave Billy time to get to know the red dragon, he was surprised at how quickly the dragon was growing. He finally decided to stay with Ruffus, as Billy couldn't pronounce his dragon name, Ruffus was the nearest he could get to it.

By the time all the work on Billy's home was complete, Ruffus was nearly full grown. Billy had got to know the other dragons very well too, all twenty of them, sorry, twenty one with Ruffus. Because, that was all that was left of these magnificent creatures around here. They said, from ancient tales, there could be more of their kind, in some other out of the way places.

Ruffus still being young was very careless about concealing himself, Billy was always reminding him the danger of being seen by other humans. "What *about Sid?*", asked Ruffus. "Sid's the exception and maybe one other person, I've known for a long time", said Billy. *"Who's that?"*, Ruffus asked, hoping to learn something about Billy's past.

"Ted, someone I used to call old Ted. Come to think of it, I don't really think he was that old. He kind of looked out for me, after all my family were killed in the war. He too suffered from the war, they say he was one of five people who survived, when their block of houses was bombed. He used to be a professor at a college, but he moved to London and became a recluse".

"What's a professor, what's a college. what's a war and what's bombed, where's London?" Ruffus fired one question after another at Billy. "If you'll give me a chance I'll tell you, but you may not like some of the answers".

"London, well that's a big city in the south of England and before you ask, a city is where lots of people live. England is where we all are now. Wars are nasty things, where people from different lands fight one another and lots of people die. Colleges are where people go to learn things and are taught by professors".

"Why are there wars?" asked Ruffus. "One land, or country, has got what another country wants, and some of the people in that country, hate the people in the other country. These people think they are better than the other country and wants to tell them what to do. There are hundreds of other reasons, there are wars. While some

countries want to rule over others, there will always be wars", said Billy.

"Billy what's recluse?", asked Ruffus. "That's someone who wants to be left alone", said Billy. "I think Ted and I were good for one another, we gave each other a reason to carry on". *"I like this Ted, I would like to meet him, he sounds a very nice person"*, said Ruffus. "He's a very nice person, in fact I miss him a lot", said Billy. "Next time Sid's here, I'll join him on his boat back to London, I'll try to persuade Ted to come up for a visit".

Just over a fortnight later, Billy was sitting in Ted's room trying hard to persuade him to come with him to meet Ruffus. Ted told him, he couldn't, he just didn't feel safe out of London. Billy said, "Look Ted if it weren't for you, I don't think I would be here now. You're the one who saved my life. Ruffus badly wants to meet you and I want you to meet Ruffus. I look upon Ruffus as a brother and I look upon you as a father. I would like for us to meet up together. Now, we know Ruffus can't come down to London, you'll have to come up to the Dales, it's the only way. Come on think about it, what have you got to lose? See this piece of egg I'm wearing round my neck. Since I put it on, my whole life has turned around for the good. Put it on, it can be your good luck talisman, nothing can harm you. When the boats ready to leave for Skipton, promise you'll be on it. If not for me, please do it for yourself".

"Billy when you're older, you should go into politics. I'll come, I won't need your egg piece, when the boats ready I'll be on it, that's a promise. Come on let's look over the books and see how the business is doing", said Ted. When they'd finished looking over the books. Billy went out to make a phone call to Mr McColl, the solicitor, to arrange a meeting.

The next day he was in the solicitor's office, "Now young William, what can I do for you?". "All this money, there's more than I'll ever need, I'd like to see some of it put to good use. There are still a lot of people who have been affected by the war. What if there was somewhere they could go, and talk to someone. Could you arrange something and see to the running of it", said Billy. "Well, the first thing we need to do is set up a trust fund. I think instead of a large building in one place, how about a number of smaller places spread around London. This city is very big, so places that are more local, would be better", said Mr McColl.

"Right then do what you have to, I'll sign anything", said Billy, "for er-r whatever". "Power of Attorney, William", said the solicitor. "Do what must be done, to see that it's run properly. I have more than enough to do, with my own business picking up". "If it's possible, please try to keep my name out of it. I'd like to remain what do you call it? anonymous. See I'm picking up big words", said Billy, with a little laugh.

"May I shake your hand William". "Why?", said Billy. "Because it's not every day, I get to meet a real live Philanthropist", said the solicitor. "With a big name like that, it's got to be something important", said Billy. "Here's my hand, by the way what is your name?" "Allan", "Right put it there Allan" they both shook hands.

"It'll take a couple of days to sort the paperwork out William". "That's alright, I'll be in London for at least another ten days. The names Billy". "William, we are discussing business so I will keep it formal", "Alright Allan just as you say, I should say Mr McColl as its business. I've got to get back, let me know when the paperwork is ready, goodbye Allan".

Billy was just stepping onto the dock at Skipton and turned to Ted and said, "Well it wasn't that bad, was it?". "There were a few times I had panic attacks, funny though, when I went to the bow and sat by the shell, it had a calming effect", said Ted. "Well, I did tell you, but you wouldn't listen", said Billy.

"Right, you two, we can't stand here talking all day. Come on let's go up to the warehouse", said Sid. They all made their way up to the warehouse. They sat up in the office; toasting large doorstops over the open fire, then spread them with butter. They waited until things quietened down before moving up to the Dales.

Around midnight Sid set off in the wagon with Billy and Ted, from the warehouse in Canal Street. They turned up Bay Horse Yard, then turned left into the High Street, over Mill Bridge. Then they went along Rakes Road, and took the left fork into Grassington Road, crossed over the A65, and continued to go north towards Threapland. From there they went past Hawkswicks, to Weston Fell, then on through Hawes, towards Sedbergh, then turning off about two thirds of the way into Baugh Fell. This was where Billy had built his new home.

Ruffus was there to greet them, Sid said hello to Ruffus. Billy then introduced Ted to Ruffus. They then all set to unloading the wagon. When they were done, Sid then made his way back to the warehouse. So as to be there in the morning, when his workers turned up for work. He told them he'd be back in a month to pick them up.

Ted got to know Ruffus very well, using Billy as an interpreter. He met most of the other dragons too, and was amazed at how polite and intelligent they were. They had a soothing effect on Ted, soon most of his anxiety and depressions disappeared. Ted said he hadn't felt so good in a long time. In fact, he thought, he might take up teaching again, only thought mind you. With his depressions gone, it seemed his appearance was much younger too.

Billy and Ted roamed the dales with the dragons, discovering all the wonderful scenery. One day Ted took Billy and Ruffus to one side, "You two are going to have to think about what you're going to do. Billy, are you going to spend the rest of your life up here as a hermit? Or are you going to retain a working interest in the company. If so, it will mean occasionally, you two having to part company, for short periods of time, when you have to go down to London. I know you're coping at the moment, but these periods may get longer, how are the pair of you going to cope?"

"Don't worry Ted, while I was down in London, I occasionally felt Ruffus's thoughts, very faint I'll grant you, but as he gets older, I think our contact will get much stronger", said Billy, "so I can't see any worries there". "Another thing, now that the wars over, there are more cars on the road. I can see a time when this area will be overcrowded with humans", said Ted. "Yes", said Billy, "some of the dragons have noticed that too. It's something they're looking into, but for the time being things are alright". "As long as you all don't lose sight of the possible danger", said Ted. "Don't forget; that Sid will be here tomorrow".

On his next visit to London, Billy popped in to see his solicitor. "Allan, this is not a visit on my behalf, well only in around about way. You see I'd like to know who owns the Yorkshire Dales. What is the likelihood of building work taking place in that area?" "Well, I think I can fill you in on this quite easily with no problems," said Allan. "The Yorkshire Dales are national park lands. To answer your second question, apart from in the villages on that land, there is little chance of any building being done there. Does that put your mind at rest, William?". "Yes, thank you Allan, it helps very much".

"Now, can you tell me, what all this is about?". "Sorry Allan, but I'm afraid this is one secret that will have to remain a secret", said Billy. "Maybe one day I might be able to let you know". "Very well William, I shall wait with bated breath. How about a spot of lunch", said Allan, "there's a nice little coffee and pie stall, down by the law courts". "I don't mind if I do Allan, shall we go". They both left the office and made their way to the law courts.

Over the next four years, Billy's company grew. He was spending more time with Ruffus, so there appeared to be a conflict of interest forming. He decided to leave the company to Sid and Ted. "You can't just give us the company", said Sid, "we'll have to pay you something for it". "Nonsense Sid, I'm nineteen now nearly a man, I've made up my mind. You showed me a great kindness when we first came up here, and I've never forgotten that. Ted's always been like a dad to me. The company's yours and Ted's, all I ask is that when I need to go anywhere, I can hop on one of your boats", Billy said. "Besides with my inheritance, I've got more money than I need, so there's nothing else to be said". Billy started to leave, then he turned and said, "I'll be off to the Dales" and left the office warehouse.

Billy spent more and more time at his house with Ruffus. While he was there, he changed the course of the steam, and had it flow through the cave. He upgraded his electrical system, bought two new generators and installed a water turbine to replace the waterwheel. All this happening just after he had turned twenty one. As well as visiting Skipton occasionally or going down to London.

Ted took up teaching again, not at college but at a small school on the edge of the Yorkshire Dales in Sedbergh. While still looking after the company finances, this suited him well. Sid had so many boats now, he had to hire more people, and rent more warehouses to store all his cargo. Allan even ventured up to Skipton a few times, and was let into the secret of Ruffus and the dragons. He said, "As your solicitor, your secret is safe with me".

Around this time Ruffus developed a new skill, he could move from one place to another in the blink of an eye. You know like they do in 'Star Trek'. Billy decided to use this skill to hunt around for a more secluded place, He was a little worried because more visitors were coming to the Dales, this could prove to be very awkward. He could not be sure of their reaction, to meeting a dragon in the flesh. So, they travelled all over the place looking for a new home. He found that Ruffus could also move other things as well.

Occasionally they came across other groups of dragons, who at first were suspicious of a human and dragon partnership, it was unheard of. There was also the history of the dragon's persecution by humans. Billy's charm and explanation of what they were doing, soon won them over.

Billy promised to let them know if they were successful. The only place that seemed suitable for them, was right up in the north of Scotland. Billy told Ruffus to pick up some dragons from home, and from the places where they had found other dragons. Then bring them up to Scotland, to let them see for themselves. Most of the dragons agreed to move there.

Some of the older ones said they were too old to move from where they had lived all their lives. Billy said that would be alright, he and Ruffus could keep an eye on them. In time all the other dragons moved to Scotland. Billy found a nice little cave and made himself cosy and comfortable.

Sid married a local lass and raised a family, two boys and a girl. Even Ted met someone in the twilight of his life and settled down. Billy used to visit them on a regular basis and sometimes popped down to visit Allan. He also kept an eye on the old dragons that stayed behind.

It's said that dragons have a sense of humour, and I think it's true, they're always talking about visiting their cousin in Loch Ness. And Ruffus spent a lot of time searching the loch, until he realised that he was having his leg pulled.

Billy and Ruffus shared a great life together, they travelled the world all be it secretly. They met other dragon groups along the way. Ruffus was asked to bread with many young females, to produce more of his kind. The success rate was seventy five percent, with some of them producing other odd little quirks which I haven't got time to go into now.

They say that man's time on this Earth is three score and ten, that's seventy to you and me. Billy lived until he was one hundred and thirty, alas dragons live much, much longer. Ruffus spent the remainder of his life teaching his sons and daughters and their offspring how to handle this skill that they had inherited.

Sometimes in the night, when you hear a roar of wind, it could just be one of Ruffus's offspring's flying past, when they think no one is around.

The End